BOOM TOWN

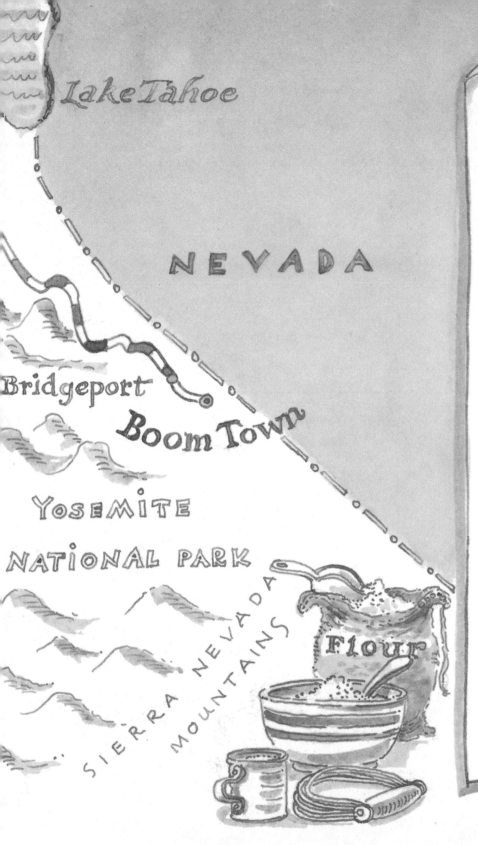

Lake Tahoe

NEVADA

Bridgeport

Boom Town

YOSEMITE

NATIONAL PARK

SIERRA NEVADA MOUNTAINS

Flour

Amanda's Gooseberry Pie

FILLING:
1 pint (2 cups) gooseberries
1 cup sugar
4 tablespoons tapioca or flour
1 teaspoon cinnamon

Use standard two-crust pie dough recipe.

Clean berries and remove stems. Combine sugar, cinnamon, and tapioca or flour and sprinkle on top of berries. Let stand at least two hours.

Preheat oven to 350°.

Take two-thirds of the dough and roll it out on a floured board, rotating it so that it forms a circle. Lift the dough gently with a spatula and place it in a greased pie pan. Press the upper edges into the side of the pie pan. Dough should extend about $1/2$ inch over the edge. Prick the bottom with a fork. Fill the pie shell with the berries. Roll out the remaining dough. Cut $1/2$-inch strips and lay the strips over the top of the berries in a crisscross design. Press the edges together.
Bake in oven at 350° for 30 minutes. Turn down oven to 325°, and bake 20 minutes more.

Makes one 8-inch pie.

BOOM TOWN

by Sonia Levitin ◉ illustrated by Cat Bowman Smith

SCHOLASTIC INC.
New York Toronto London Auckland Sydney
Mexico City New Delhi Hong Kong

For Lloyd, with love —S.L.

Dedicated to all who believe and inform . . .
"lest we forget our past." —C.B.S.

ISBN 0-439-06309-4

Text copyright © 1998 by Sonia Levitin.
Illustrations copyright © 1998 by Cat Bowman Smith.
All rights reserved. Published by Scholastic Inc., 555 Broadway,
New York, NY 10012, by arrangement with Orchard Books.
SCHOLASTIC and associated logos are trademarks and/or regis-
tered trademarks of Scholastic Inc.

12 11 10 9 8 7 6 5 4 3 2   1 2 3 4 5/0

Printed in the U.S.A.   08

First Scholastic printing, March 2000

The text of this book is set in 17 point Cheltenham Old Style.
The illustrations are in watercolor.

It took us twenty-one days on the stagecoach to get to California. When we got there, I thought we'd live with Pa in the gold fields. A whole tent city was built up. But Ma shook her head. "The gold fields are no place for children. We'll get a cabin and live in town."

What town? A stage stop, a pump house, a few log cabins—that was all. It was so wide and lonesome out west, even my shadow ran off.

Ma found a cabin big enough for all of us: Baby Betsy, brothers Billy, Joe, Ted, and me—Amanda. Pa came in from the gold fields every Saturday night, singing:

"So I got me a mule
And some mining tools,
A shovel and a pick and pan;

But I work all day
Without no pay.
I guess I'm a foolish man."

First Ma made him take a bath in a tin tub set out under the stars. Then Pa sang songs and told stories he'd heard from the miners—stories about men finding big nuggets and striking it rich. But poor Pa, he had no luck at all. Still, every Monday morning he'd leave for the gold fields full of hope.

Days were long and lonely. The hills spread out as far as forever. Nights, me and Ma and my brothers and Baby Betsy would sit out and wait for a shooting star to sail across the sky. Once in a while a crow flew by. That's all the excitement there was.

My brothers worked up some furrows. They planted corn and potatoes and beans. Then they ran around climbing trees, skinning their knees. But after all the water was fetched and the wash was done, after the soap was made and the fire laid, after the beds were fixed and the floor was swept clean, I'd sit outside our cabin door with Baby Betsy, so bored I thought I'd die. Also, I hankered for some pie. I loved to bake pie.

I asked Ma and she said, "Pie would be good, but we have no pie pans and no real oven, just the wood stove. How would you bake a pie?"

I poked around in a big box of stuff and found an old iron skillet. I decided to make a pie crust and pick gooseberries to fill it.

Gooseberries grew on the bushes near town. I picked a big pailful and went back home. I made a crust with flour, butter, a little water, and a pinch of salt, and then I rolled it out.

Ma came in and said, "Looks good, Amanda. I knew you could make it. But tell me, how will you bake it?"

I showed Ma the skillet. She shook her head. "I don't think it will work, but you can try."

"It will work," I said.

Brothers Billy and Joe and Ted stood there laughing. When the wood turned to coals, I pushed my pie inside the old stove. After a while I smelled a bad burning. I pulled out my pie, hard as a rock. Billy, Joe, and Ted whooped and slapped their sides. They snatched up my pie and tossed it high into the air. They ran outside and Billy whacked it hard with a stick. Pie pieces flew all over the place, and my brothers bent over, laughing.

I was so mad I went right back in to make another, and I swore none of them would get a bite. I rolled out my crust and filled it with berries, shoved the pie into the oven, and soon took it out.

I set the pie down to cool. I went off to do some mending. Next thing I knew, Baby Betsy, just learning to walk, sat there with pie goo all over her face. Too soft, the filling ran down on Betsy, and she wailed like a coyote in the night.

It took one more try, but I got it right. That night we ate my gooseberry pie, and it was delicious.

When Pa came home from the gold fields on Saturday night, there was a pie for him, too. "Amanda, you are the queen of the kitchen!" Pa scooped me up and whirled me around. I was proud.

The next week I made an extra pie for Pa to take with him to the gold fields.

Saturday night when he came home singing, coins jangled in his pocket.
We all ran out to ask, "Did you strike gold, Pa?"
"No," he said. "I sold Amanda's pie. The miners loved it. They paid me
twenty-five cents a slice!"

After that, Pa took pies to the gold fields every week. And every week he came home with coins in his pockets. Some miners walked right to our door looking for pie. They told Ma, "You should open a bakery."

Ma said, "It's my girl Amanda who is the baker. If she wants to make pies, that's fine. But I have no time."

Ma had a new baby on the way. It was up to me. I figured I could sell pies to the miners and fill up our money jar.

But I needed help. I rounded up my brothers and told them, "If you want to eat pie, you've got to work."

They grumbled and groaned, but they knew I meant it. So Billy built me a shelf, Joe made a sign, AMANDA'S FINE PIES, and Ted helped pick berries and sour apples.

I needed more pans and another bucket. One day Peddler Pete came by, and with the money I'd made I bought them.

"You're a right smart little girl," said the peddler, "being in business like this."

I thought fast and told him, "Anybody can make money out here. Folks need things all the time, and there're no stores around. If you were to settle and start one, I'll bet you'd get rich."

Peddler Pete scratched his beard. "Not a bad idea," he said. "My feet are sore from roaming. I could use this cart and build my way up to having a store."

So pretty soon we had us a real store called PEDDLER PETE'S TRADING POST. Trappers and traders and travelers appeared. After shopping at Pete's, they were good and hungry.

They came to our cabin, looking for pie. Some liked it here so well they decided to stay. Soon we had a cooper, a tanner, a miller, a blacksmith. A town was starting to grow.

A prospector came in on the stage from St. Joe, his clothes covered with dirt.
He looked around at the folks eating pie, and he asked, "Is there someone here
who does washing?"

I stepped right up and I told him, "What we need is a laundry. Why don't
you stay and start one? Why, the miners are sending their shirts clear to China.
You'll make more money doing laundry than looking for gold."

The man thought a while, then said with a smile, "You're right, little lady.
It's a dandy idea. I'll send for my wife to help."

Soon shirts and sheets fluttered on the line as people brought their washing in. A tailor came to make and mend clothes. A cobbler crafted shoes and boots. We heard the *tap tap* of his hammer and smelled the sweet leather. A barber moved in with shaving mugs, and an apothecary with herbs and healing drugs. So the town grew up all around us.

My pie business blossomed. Sometimes the line snaked clear around the house. Baby Betsy entertained the people while they waited. Billy added another shelf. Joe and Ted made a bench. We all picked berries and apples. Even Ma came to help. We had to get a bigger jar for all the money coming in.

One day our old friend Cowboy Charlie rode by. Like everyone else, he stopped for some pie. "I'd like to rest a spell," he said. "Where can I leave my horse for the night?"

"There's no livery stable," I said. "But why don't you start one? You'd rent out horses, and wagons too. That would be a perfect business for you."

"You're just full of great ideas, little lady," Cowboy Charlie said. He twirled his lariat. "I'd like to settle down. I'll stay here and do just that."

Soon a trail was worn right to Charlie's stable door. All day we heard the snorting of horses. Now Charlie needed hay. Farmers brought wagons and sacks full of feed. With all those people riding in, someone decided to build a hotel and a cafe. The town grew fast all around us.

The owner of the cafe bought pies from me, five or six at a time. I taught Billy how to roll the crust. Joe got wood for the stove. Ted washed the fruit, and Baby Betsy tried to stir in the sugar.

The money jar in our kitchen looked ready to bust. Where could we safely keep all that cash? Lucky us, one day Mr. Hooper, the banker, appeared.

"I'm building a bank," Mr. Hooper said to me. "This is getting to be a boom town."

"We'll use your bank," I told Mr. Hooper, "but the roads are so poor. In winter there's mud, and in summer there's dust. We need some sidewalks and better streets."

"You're a smart little lady," said Mr. Hooper, tipping his hat. "I'll see what I can do about that."

Before we knew it, the bank was built and wooden sidewalks were laid. One street was called Bank Street; the other was Main. Soon every lane and landmark had a name. Pa and my brothers built on a big room for our bakery.

Men sent for their families. New houses appeared everywhere. Babies and children filled up the town. We needed a school, and a good schoolmarm.

We knew Miss Camilla from our stagecoach days. She was living up the coast
a ways. Cowboy Charlie rode off to fetch her, and she was glad to come.

Miss Camilla, the teacher, had married a preacher, and he came too. We all
got together to build a church and a school. Bells rang out every day of the
week. Now this was a real boom town!

One day Pa said to me, "Amanda, I'm through panning for gold. Will you let me be in business with you?"

"Sure!" I said, happily. "I'd love to work with you, Pa, and I'd also like to go to school."

So Pa turned to baking, and we all worked together. Pa sang while he rolled out the dough:

> "Amanda found a skillet
> And berries to fill it,
> Made pies without a pan;
>
> Our pies are the best
> In all the West.
> I guess I'm a lucky man."

Now Pa is with us every day. There's excitement and bustle all around. Our house sits in the middle of a boom town!

And to think it all started with me, Amanda, baking pies!

HISTORICAL NOTE

When gold was discovered in the West, thousands of people came to join the Gold Rush, hoping to get rich. Most were disappointed. It was not so easy to find gold. But many made fortunes by opening stores and providing things that the miners and their families needed.

"A young lady who learned to improvise baked $11,000 worth of pies in a small iron skillet."* This book is dedicated to her and to all the resourceful and hardworking people who built the West.

*From *California: A History of the Golden State* by Warren A. Beck and David A. Williams, Doubleday, 1972.

Lake Tahoe

NEVADA

Bridgeport

Boom Town

Yosemite

National Park

Sierra Nevada Mountains

Flour

Amanda's Gooseberry Pie

FILLING:
1 pint (2 cups) gooseberries
1 cup sugar
4 tablespoons tapioca or flour
1 teaspoon cinnamon

Use standard two-crust pie dough recipe.

Clean berries and remove stems. Combine sugar, cinnamon, and tapioca or flour and sprinkle on top of berries. Let stand at least two hours.

Preheat oven to 350°.

Take two-thirds of the dough and roll it out on a floured board, rotating it so that it forms a circle. Lift the dough gently with a spatula and place it in a greased pie pan. Press the upper edges into the side of the pie pan. Dough should extend about ½ inch over the edge. Prick the bottom with a fork. Fill the pie shell with the berries. Roll out the remaining dough. Cut ½-inch strips and lay the strips over the top of the berries in a crisscross design. Press the edges together.
Bake in oven at 350° for 30 minutes. Turn down oven to 325°, and bake 20 minutes more.

Makes one 8-inch pie.